FAUN
THE NAUG

Faun and the naughtiest pig

Anne Townsend

Illustrations
Eileen Bazire

OMF BOOKS LONDON

© OVERSEAS MISSIONARY FELLOWSHIP

First published February 1974

ISBN 85363 093 3

Made in Great Britain
Published by Overseas Missionary Fellowship
Newington Green, London, N16 9QD
and printed by Emprint, Whitstable, Kent CT5 1AG

FOR JANET, DAVID AND CHRISTOPHER

In case you want to know

Faun and his mother and the pig family, and the Townsends too, are all real. Most of the things that happen to them in this book really happened, but a few things are extra. The story cannot be finished because when this was written in 1972, the events of the last chapter had just taken place. Whether Faun lives happily ever after or not perhaps depends on *you* remembering to pray for him sometimes.

CONTENTS

Chapter		Page
1	The Naughtiest Pig	11
2	More Trouble	16
3	Kite Fight	20
4	Hallo God!	24
5	Everything Changes	29
6	Who Wants a Boy?	35

'Jon! For goodness sake stop!'

CHAPTER ONE

THE NAUGHTIEST PIG

FAUN felt his heart might burst, it was thumping so hard.

'Jon!' he yelled down the path, 'For goodness sake stop!'

He seemed to have been running for ever. It was no good. He knew that the littlest pig, who had wriggled out from under the bamboo fence enclosing the pigs, was enjoying this chase. It was not going to give up its freedom without a struggle. Faun knew he faced another race before he would be able to catch the piglet, tie some raffia around his neck, and lead him home to where he belonged with the rest of the pig family.

He ran as fast as his eight year-old legs would go, beginning to sense an empty feeling in his stomach. He had already boiled up the rice ready for his evening meal. The rice pot bubbled and boiled on a clay bucket filled with glowing charcoal, set on the floor of the wooden house. He had to be careful that no sparks set the small two-roomed house on fire. As it was raised up on stilts, six feet off the ground, it could easily catch alight and burn down.

He would have to wait for his mother to come home from work at sunset. She would make delicious curries and Thai stews to have with the rice. Then he could eat his fill. Meanwhile, he must catch Jon. He would be in for trouble if the naughtiest, littlest pig was missing when she reached home. Raising the pig family was one of the many ways in which his mother earned extra money for him to go to the best school in their village in Central Thailand. He knew that he must have once had a father, but his mother never spoke about him and so Faun had learnt to ask no questions. This meant that he had to be the man of the house and help his mother with all the men's jobs. The two of them lived on their own, as their granny lived a long way away.

He nearly tripped over a big stone as he ran, his eyes glued to the piglet and not on the path.

'No . . . please don't!' he shouted hopelessly after the piglet. He now knew the littlest piglet well enough to realize exactly where he was heading.

'*Please* Jon, don't!' he shouted desperately.

The littlest pig gave not even a twitch of his curled-up tail in response to his master's commands. It lolloped merrily on and on. It blundered along the bumpy mud road, heading straight for the one place in all the world that Faun least wished it to visit.

The naughtiest pig was on its way to explore a *hospital*, and Faun could not stop it. He could imagine it scuttering up and down, leaving behind it a trail of muddy foot marks and an angry hospital nurse. He did not look forward to the game of hide-and-seek he knew the pig wanted to play with him around the hospital wards. However, the pig first made a bee-line straight for the out-patient department when the doctors were busy seeing patients.

Faun hid himself away behind the leaves of a big tropical tree that grew by the out-patient department. His eyes were glued on the hospital, hoping to glimpse the naughty pig through the sprays of pink flowers. He dared not go in himself because he did not want anyone to know this naughty pig had anything to do with him.

A few minutes later he spotted someone chasing the pig out. To his relief he saw that it was Doctor John, a missionary doctor from England; one with a kind face but remarkable to the Thai for his long pointed nose, so unlike Faun's little Thai snub nose.

The patients sitting waiting laughed so hard that they ached with laughing more than with the aches and pains that had brought them to the hospital. They had never seen anything as funny as this pink-skinned, yellow-haired foreigner chasing a pig in and out and around the waiting room benches. Finally they ran out into the sunshine. The patients laughed even harder as the doctor spanked the pig and said,

'Just because you and I have similar names, don't you follow me into the hospital again!'

Faun thought the pig was laughing too. Neither of them was frightened of Doctor John, even though he was a strange foreigner. Faun ran and grabbed Jon firmly by the scruff of his neck.

'How will you get him home?' the doctor asked.

Faun shrugged.

'I've an idea . . .' The doctor disappeared and fetched an old crepe bandage. They tied it round Jon's neck like a collar and lead.

To make quite sure that he would not lose Jon again, Faun tied the end of the bandage around his own right wrist. As soon as the pig felt the bandage go slack, it had another idea.

It ran hard, dragging Faun behind it. This time it knew it would be all right. He could see that the pig was heading for Doctor John's house, where Faun's mother worked. He liked going there. Doctor John and his wife, Doctor Anne, were new missionaries in Thailand. Doctor Anne had no idea how to clean her Thai house the way that Thai people did, nor how to manage all the washing in bowls of cold water on the verandah, nor even how to cook proper Thai food. He had once politely forced himself to eat the rice she had cooked herself, and privately thought that no self-respecting Thai person could ever live on rice as soggy and tasteless as hers. He was proud and glad that his mother helped her run a Thai home properly. This gave Doctor Anne time to learn to speak his Thai language and also look after some of the patients who came to the hospital.

Best of all, he was glad that she often invited him to come and play with her children, Janet and David, after school.

On Sundays, his mother's day off, he was sometimes invited to the doctor's house to eat the funny mid-day

Faun . . . tied the pig firmly to one of the wooden posts.

meal that Doctor Anne cooked and called 'Sunday roast' ... he really preferred his rice and curries.

Jon tugged Faun, dragging him firmly towards the mud surrounding the concrete patch under the doctor's house. Faun slipped the bandage off his wrist and tied the pig firmly to one of the high wooden posts on which the little house perched ten feet up off the ground.

He quietly climbed up the wooden stairs and peeped inside the front door to see if anything interesting was happening.

CHAPTER TWO

MORE TROUBLE

AS soon as he peeped inside the ever-open front door it was obvious that he was wanted.

Baby David crawled towards him, a smile lighting up his face, and stretching from ear to ear in welcome. He put up his arms expecting his customary cuddle from his best friend.

Faun had never known anything in the world quite like this foreign baby. He never ceased to marvel at the skin as pale as that of the most beautiful Thai women; the eyes as blue as the kingfishers darting to and fro in the rice fields; and the extraordinary hair, the russet brown colour of the robes worn by a few special elderly Buddhist monks. This baby was so unlike the bronze-skinned Thai babies with their black hair and brown eyes. Faun loved and cared for this baby, like the baby brother he had never had.

He was proud that Doctor Anne trusted him enough to let him look after her baby on his own, under the house where it was often cooler than inside the house. He picked up the baby and carried him downstairs, settling him on a mat on the cement, surrounded by his toys.

However, he soon saw that today was not going to be as easy as usual. The pig was causing nothing but trouble today. The baby saw Jon and Jon saw the baby.

Faun had a sinking feeling that Doctor Anne would not want her baby playing with a *pig*, but that soon he would be unable to prevent this very thing from happening. He tried to distract Jon by throwing him some food scraps and to gain the baby's attention by

Jon . . . fell flat on his side, right by the baby's feet.

playing 'peep-bo' with him.

His efforts were wasted. They were irresistibly drawn together. Within seconds Jon had strained so hard at his bandage leash that it suddenly snapped and he fell flat on his side, right by the baby's feet. David chuckled with glee at the muddy piglet sprawling in front of him. What a wonderful new toy his friend Faun had brought for him to play with today! He stretched out his little hand to grab the pig's tail, to put it in his mouth. What did pigs' tails taste of, he wondered.

'David! Stop it!' came a command from above.

All eyes were drawn upwards by Doctor Anne's voice, and all met her glare. Faun could not decide whether she was amused or upset. All that he knew was that he must remove his grubby pig quickly from the baby, and make sure that it never visited the Townsend house again, or he would be in for a ticking-off from his mother.

Doctor Anne lifted David up, and carried him into the house. Faun firmly and reluctantly led his naughty pig home.

He patched the hole in the fence with pieces of bamboo, so that Jon could not wriggle out again. Then he decided to return to the Townsend house. Perhaps he could play with Janet until his own mother was ready to come home.

He walked back. As he walked he remembered six months ago when he had first visited the Townsends. He had been most puzzled. Doctors Anne and John had both been given Thai names and were known as 'Anong' and 'Jeroon' by the Thai. When Faun had first visited their house, he had been bewildered because Doctor Anong kept on calling for his *naughty pig*.

She would shout out in English, 'John . . . John . . .'

This, of course, was the name of Faun's littlest pig, 'Jon'. It took him weeks to realize that Doctor 'Jeroon's' *English* name was *John* — the same pronunciation as Faun's *Jon*. Faun discovered that Doctor Anne was calling for *her* husband and not for *his* pig.

By the time he reached the Townsend house again, the family was having supper. He sat out on the cool verandah watching the Thai people in the houses round about having their evening baths by the wells. The ladies tucked their tube-like sarongs under their arms and bathed inside this cylinder of cloth, pouring cool water over themselves. They then drew a clean, dry sarong over their heads, and slipped off the wet one when the dry one was almost in place.

As he had hoped, Janet had already left the table early and came and joined him on the verandah with a pile of books. She was four years old and looked to him like a giant walking, talking imitation of the pink plastic dolls for sale in the local market. Next to the baby, she was the second wonder of his life. She would have seemed unreal to him, except that he had seen her cry when hurt, laugh when amused, sometimes be cross and sometimes be kind. What was more she was learning to speak his language and so he knew that this was no *doll*. This was a real child, as real as any little Thai girl.

Her books fascinated him. He had never held books so heavy or thick before. They contained pictures that he thought must be the most beautiful in all the world. In many of them he discovered pictures of a strong kind man with long hair and white clothes. Janet told him stories about this man as they went from picture to picture. She explained that this man was called 'Jesus', and had been alive two thousand years ago. Faun used to think that when she talked about Him it seemed as if she believed that He was still alive today. Yet he knew that this must be nonsense because in other pictures she had shown this Jesus dying on a cross. It was too much of a muddle for him to understand and Janet was too young to explain everything that he wanted to know. He loved the hours they spent together poring over these fascinating pictures.

'Time to go!' His mother interrupted them.

She handed him a big tin, full of left-over food slops. They would carry it home as supper for Jon and the rest of the pig family.

Faun jumped up. Now he remembered how hungry he was. Soon he would get his supper.

Next, it was going to be tomorrow; and tomorrow was the very special day when there was to be the kite-flying competition.

'Bye-bye, Janet!' he shouted, using the few English words he knew. He was unable to wave, because of the heavy tin of food slops in his arms. 'Ask your mother if you can come to the kite-fight tomorrow,' he added in Thai.

'I'll take you both,' offered Doctor John.

Faun had felt that the kite-day would never even come.

Now it was to be as soon as tomorrow *and* he was going with both Janet and Doctor John.

19

CHAPTER THREE

KITE FIGHT

THE day dragged on endlessly. Faun thought that the early evening would never be reached.

He knew that the kite contest would not begin until evening, when the blazing sun began to sink towards the horizon, tinting the clouds with pink and purple glory. Once the sun began to go down the evening breezes would gently rustle the leaves of the trees in the rice fields. The rustle would gradually change to a faint roar, as the wind gained speed. This was the time of day for playing kites.

At long last a breeze began to flicker the leaves of the Flame of the Forest tree shading his home.

He hurried to the Townsends' home.

'It's time!' he called out excitedly.

Janet and Doctor John appeared at the top of the stairs.

'O.K. We'll go now,' the doctor replied in Thai.

He wheeled his bicycle to the end of the path leading to the house. He then sat Janet on a tiny seat fixed behind the handle bars, while Faun perched side-saddle on the back carrier.

Faun was half proud and half embarrassed to be seen going out with foreigners like this. Heads were turned to gaze at the doctor, and especially at his doll-like daughter. When spoken to, this 'doll' replied in fluent Thai, which so amazed the questioners that many were left speechless. She spoke Thai better than her father.

Faun knew that he himself would meet a non-stop stream of questions. Doctor John was always asking about Thailand and wanting to understand Thai customs and ways of doing things. So Faun tried to remember all that the old people had told him about kite flying.

One old granny had declared that kite competitions started about six hundred years ago. Later, about the year 1689, a big town had rebelled against the king. The king's army could not quell the riot. So the following year explosives were tied to the strings of kites and flown over the rebelling town. Many of the wooden houses rapidly burnt down and there was so much chaos that the town was forced to surrender to the king. These ancient kites were given the name 'Chula' kites.

As Faun was remembering these stories the doctor slowed his bicycle to a halt. He lifted the two children down and they joined a crowd watching a contest between two kite-fighters.

A big kite and a smaller one were hovering 'way up in the sky, locked together, each trying to fell the other.

Faun began to tell the doctor all he knew about these kites.

'The big one is called "Chula",' he began. 'That's a male one. The smaller female is called "Pakpao". The winner is the person who pulls the other kite down on to his half of the ground.'

'Don't people ever fix glass or something to their kite, that will ruin the other one?' Doctor John asked.

'That's forbidden. It would spoil the fun,' Faun replied.

They gazed up at the kites.

'I know what Pakpao is trying to do,' Faun spoke quickly and excitedly. 'She has a looped tail, and although she's so small, she can catch Chula if she can get his head trapped in her loop. Then she can easily pull him down to her side and win.'

They saw Pakpao succeed in doing this, and sat in the

cool of the evening watching the kites for a long time.

'Tell you a secret,' said Doctor John as he took the two children home when darkness fell, 'I've already bought Janet a Pakpao kite and Faun a Chula one. The leprosy patients in the hospital have been making and selling them. Tomorrow you can play kites yourselves.'

Faun was delighted. He had always longed for a Chula kite. He liked all the other kinds; the Tuy-tuy which sang in the wind, and the ones shaped like birds, butterflies and centipedes; but he had always longed for his very own Chula kite.

His mother was waiting for him at the Townsends' house.

'Stay for a bit and I'll tell you a story with Janet,' invited Doctor John.

Faun's mother smiled in consent. She was sitting on the front steps of the house, busy finishing some extra sewing she was doing to earn money to pay for Faun's school clothes.

The doctor then told them a story about some of Janet's pictures. He was able to explain to Faun so that he understood much more than when Janet had tried to explain. The story was about the first man and woman in the world, and where they had come from.

He explained that there was a God who made people.

Faun sat up straight to concentrate on what he was hearing. This was news to him! He had always wondered where the world had come from. He had never heard before of any God who had made anything. This story was new and interesting.

The doctor said that just as a Chula kite needed Pakpao for Thai kite games to be played properly, so *God* had made men and women to help one another. Men made kites — but God made men!

This story was news to Faun. Every time he admired

his new Chula kite, he thought about the story of a God who had made the men who could make things like kites.

If there was such a Being as a God who had created everything, then it made sense of the world and how it had come into being.

Faun returned home that night not only with a new kite but with something new to think about.

'I've bought Janet a Pakpao kite & Faun a Chula one.'

CHAPTER FOUR

HALLO GOD!

TWO years passed and the Townsends and Faun grew older.

'The trouble with you is that you'll be a Christian before very long!' Faun's mother exclaimed one day.

He knew his mother's words were true. Deep down in his heart he *did* believe in the God of the Christians and he was beginning to love the Lord Jesus for himself.

It was not only Janet's pictures that had made him think about God, but he had also started going to a weekly Christian Sunday School in the market. Thai Christians and missionaries had taught him every week about a loving God who was like a Father and about His Son the Lord Jesus Christ.

One day in Sunday School Faun had asked this Lord Jesus to come and live in his heart and to be his Saviour. He had never told his mother about this, but he did not think she would really mind. She seemed halfway to doing the same thing herself.

'How would you like to leave your present school and go to a Christian boarding school?' his mother suddenly asked.

Now he could hardly believe his ears.

'Do you really mean it?' he asked, thrilled with the idea.

He had often enviously watched some of the children of the Thai Christian staff at the hospital go away to the boarding school. There they could learn every day about the Lord Jesus. He had often secretly longed that he too could go there. Now his mother was putting it forward as if it was *her* very own idea.

His mother nodded, 'Yes! I think you'd better go too ... but Jon will have to be sold. If you go to that school, then I'll need money for all your new things — and Jon is fat enough to sell for a good price now.'

Faun did not know whether to laugh or cry.

He longed to go away to this school; but he could not bear the thought of having to part with Jon.

He wandered silently down to the pig enclosure under the house, and leant against the fence staring at his friend. There was Jon. As usual he was covered in mud. Now he was so big that he could no longer qualify for the title of 'the littlest pig'; there were many baby piglets smaller than him now.

Faun thought, 'Anyway, he's still the "naughtiest pig".'

Jon playfully rolled two of the baby piglets over & over.

As if he read his master's thoughts, Jon playfully rolled two of the baby piglets over and over in the mud with his snout, waggling his ears in delight at their squeals of pleasure in the games he was playing with them.

'I love you, Jon!' Faun almost exclaimed aloud..., but stopped as soon as he realized that this would be a very stupid thing to be overheard saying to a *pig*.

'Still, it's true,' he admitted to himself, 'I *do* love Jon ... and I don't want him to have to be sold so that I can go to a new school.'

He stared sadly at the pig, wondering if there was anything he could do.

As he watched the pig's games, he remembered some words that Doctor John had prayed one Sunday lunchtime before they had begun their meal.

He had prayed something like, 'Thank you, our Father God, because You always give us the money for our food, clothes, electricity, water and for all the things that we need.'

Faun could see that this was true. God *did* give the Townsend family all that they needed.

He began to wonder, 'If God does this for my friends Janet and David, then will He do it for me too?'

The more he thought about it, the more he wanted to try it. After all, he had been told in Sunday School that everything the Bible said was meant for *him*. Parts of the Bible said that God would give Christians everything they needed. Did that apply to a little boy and his pig or not? Faun decided to try it out and see.

He fixed his eyes firmly on Jon and began to have a chat with God. He was not very good at praying to God in the proper way that grown-ups did in Thailand. They spoke to God in a very special language that was only used when talking to a member of the royal family; this was their way of being very respectful to God. Faun was no good at using this language yet, and so whenever he wanted to pray he chatted to God, trying to speak as politely as he would to the headmaster of his school.

'Good afternoon, God,' he began, 'This is me, your friend Faun, again. Please God, do you think that You can help me? You know how much I want to go to that Christian school where I can learn about You as well as doing lessons. But God, the trouble is, I don't want to go if I have to lose my friend Jon. Please God, is there anything You can do to help? Thank you very much. Goodbye.'

He wondered if he had just done something very silly. After all, why should the God who created the whole world be interested in helping one little boy to keep his pet pig ... God must have much more important things to do. He wandered upstairs again and started to chop up vegetables ready for the evening meal. His mother had gone off to work, but would be back again soon.

'You idiot,' he told himself. 'A great big strong God like that won't be bothered whether or not a ten year-old boy has his pig or not.'

He nearly chopped at his fingers instead of the vegetables, by mistake, he was feeling so stupid.

By the time his mother returned he had decided to tell her that he did not want to go away to school. He would keep Jon instead. He knew that if he parted from Jon, then the pig would land up as meat for sale in the market next week, and he could not bear to let that happen.

His mother bounced upstairs into the house. Faun was startled. She usually moved slowly and graciously, she never *bounced*.

'Faun,' she shouted loudly. 'Come here, right away.'

He moved to the verandah and looked at her face in surprise. Instead of her usual placid expression, her face was shining with delight.

'Doctor John has just said that if you go to the Christian school then you can have money from a scholarship fund to help pay your fees.'

He looked at her, hardly believing her. 'Doctor John says that there are Christians in other countries who have sent money for children like you to go to a Christian school where you can learn about God as well as learning ordinary school lessons.'

Faun swallowed hard and then took the plunge to ask the question he most wanted answered, 'What about Jon?'

'We can keep him now,' she replied lightly and happily.

He felt as if he would burst with happiness. Words came tumbling out of his mouth almost faster than he could speak them, as he shared with her his prayer to God.

'Fancy,' he finished in amazement, 'this God even loves me and Jon.'

His mother smiled one of her secret smiles so that he could not tell what she was really thinking. 'Come on, now we'll have to get busy preparing your things,' was all she said.

CHAPTER FIVE

EVERYTHING CHANGES

'I hate school!' was Faun's private reaction at first to his new school.

Everything was strange and different.

The day time wasn't too bad, except for the school food. It was the nights that were the worst. He slept in a bed on his own in a dormitory with fifteen other little boys. Always before, he and his mother had slept close, sharing the same mattress under the same mosquito net, as most Thai families did. He desperately missed his mother at night, when he woke up and found that her familiar and loved warmth and smell were absent. He would automatically put out a hand to feel for her comforting presence and find only emptiness. The unaccustomed quietness of the nights bothered him too. He had become used to sleeping through the snuffles and snorts of Jon and the pig family who lived directly under the floor of his home. At school the classroom under his dormitory was empty at night; the only sounds were the occasional eerie hooting of an owl, the scutter of rats across the wooden floor, or rare howl of a dog.

His first term away at school seemed to him to be complete misery! He was comforted a little in knowing that his English friend Janet had also gone away to boarding school. Her school, Chefoo School, was for missionaries' children and was set high up in the hills of the Cameron Highlands of West Malaysia. He did not know exactly where that was, but he knew it took Janet one day and one and a half nights to get there. He imagined that she must miss her mother as much as he did his.

The four children had hours of fun in the pond.

However, by the second term, life improved. Faun was no longer a new boy who did not know how to do anything properly. He had grown accustomed to the place and the people, and was beginning to *enjoy* himself. Even the food began to taste better.

He was now able to stop sitting, looking miserably out of the window, thinking of home, during lesson time. He began to study hard, and to his surprise he found that with a bit of effort he could always come top of his class. His mother's face radiated pride each time he presented her with his end of term report, saying that once again he had done well. The Townsend family were away in England for two years at this time, so the good news of his progress could no longer be shared with them.

When the Townsends finally returned Faun could hardly believe his eyes. His doll-like Janet was a pretty eight year-old girl, 'baby David' was a mischievous six year-old, and the latest addition to the family, Christopher, was a sturdy independent three year-old. Faun supposed that he too must look bigger and older to them! Now they could have real fun playing together.

The best fun came from old polystyrene packing cases that had been used to pack around equipment when it came to Thailand from abroad. These huge polystyrene pieces floated in water, and if a child sat inside or on them they made magnificent boats. The four children had hours of fun in the pond in the Townsends' garden with their unwieldy makeshift boats.

Faun could tell from Doctor Anne's face that she too was enjoying their fun as she sat watching them from the verandah. When the boats tipped over (usually on purpose) and the children were deposited in the waist-high water she would pretend to be cross and make them scrub the layers of mud off themselves with the garden hose before she would allow them into the house. But Faun knew that she did not really mind the mess.

'Faun . . . ,' Doctor Anne stopped him one day. 'Is your mother getting enough to eat? She looks terribly thin. Since we came back from England she hasn't seemed like her old self at all.'

He replied, 'I'm sure she's O.K.'

He had grown accustomed to seeing his mother every day in the holidays and had not noticed any change in her.

However, after Doctor Anne spoke to him, he began to watch his mother more closely. He began to see that the doctor was right. His mother *was* getting very thin, and sometimes her face crumpled up as if something was hurting deep inside her.

'What's the matter?' he asked one day, as her face began to wrinkle up, and she stopped work and bent over, breathing quickly.

'Just stomach ache . . . It'll go off in a minute; it always does,' she reassured him.

Faun believed her and returned happily to the school he now loved. He continued to do well in his lessons and found that he was growing to know the Lord Jesus more and more as a real Person, for himself. He had decided firmly that for the rest of his life he would be a Christian, until the day he died and went to be with God in Heaven.

When he returned home for the next holidays and his mother met him, he was shocked. She looked very, very ill. She was so thin now that she tried to make a joke out of it.

'If you look at me sideways you can't see me now!' She tried to smile. It was no good, Faun could not laugh, he was too upset to see how thin she had become.

He was no longer fooled by her attempts to pretend

that she was all right. He could see for himself that there was something seriously wrong with his mother.

When she quietly told him one night that she was going to have an operation the next week, he was not at all surprised. He accompanied her to the hospital and, as is the custom at the Christian hospital at Manorom, he stayed with her all the time. At night he slept on the floor under her bed, and during the day he helped the nurses make her comfortable.

Sometimes she would say, 'I'm going to sleep now, you run and play with the Townsends.'

His feet would drag in the direction of the Townsend house. He would go to the pond and the boats, but it was all fun no longer. Deep inside himself, after his mother's operation, he knew that she was never going to get better. Maybe it was the look in her eyes that told him what she knew; maybe it was the hours she spent talking to the doctors; or maybe it was that every day she seemed to get thinner and thinner. Whatever it was, he knew that she would not get better.

When the 'great day' came for her to be discharged from hospital and go home, Faun found that it was not a 'great day' at all. She was so weak that she could not even walk up the stairs of their home and had to be carried up by neighbours. Faun had to do everything for her.

'The pigs will have to go,' she gently said to him one day.

This time he knew that she was right. He wept silently in bed that night, knowing that his friend Jon would have to go.

When the men came to collect the pigs, Faun made sure that he was away in the market so that he would never have to say goodbye to Jon.

He felt that he could not bear to have to face the parting. When he returned from the market Jon had

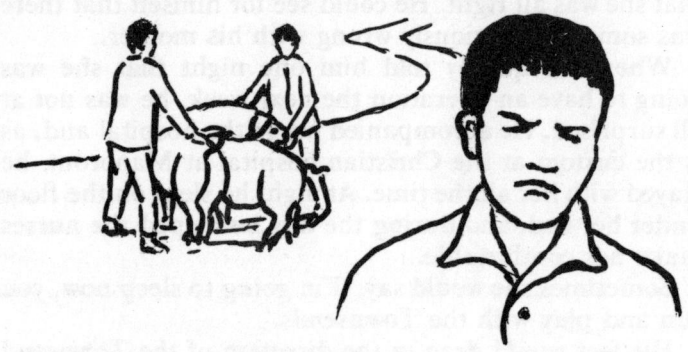

He felt that he could not bear to have to face the parting.

disappeared. He tried not to cry and add to his mother's troubles.

When she quietly explained that she was selling their home and that they would move to another town to live with her mother, he knew that this too was the right thing to do. He, a twelve year-old now, could not manage everything in the house on his own.

His heart was breaking.

His home and loved pig family were gone ... and one day soon, he knew, his mother would die.

CHAPTER SIX

WHO WANTS A BOY?

THE problem that constantly bothered Faun was more to do with his mother than to do with himself.

He knew that he would miss her deeply when she died, but he had been taught to try and control his feelings, as all Thai children are. He did not know what would happen to him once she had gone or where he would live. Yet, the thing that constantly gnawed at his heart was the fact that although his mother had often heard about the God of Christianity, his very own God now, yet she had never truly trusted in Him.

As she lay weakly in his granny's house and he fetched and carried for her, they chatted together for hours. She shared all the wisdom she had accumulated in her life, and wanted to pass on to her son. She made him promise to be upright, honest, always to study hard, and to try and make something worthwhile of his life. She told him that there was a little money put by in the bank from the sale of the pigs and the house that was for him later on when he needed it.

Sometimes as they sat quietly together, watching the tiny house-lizards scurrying over the walls in the evenings, their tongues darting out like flames to catch insects, they would talk about the thing that most concerned Faun. He was now able to tell his mother about the Lord Jesus and how much he had come to love Him. Somehow, he knew that this time it would *not* be right for him to ask God to make his mother better. It wasn't that God *couldn't*; Faun knew that He *could*; but he sensed that God was going to allow his mother to die,

35

and he felt strangely peaceful about it. He often asked God to help his mother to understand, and to meet with God for herself before she died. He knew that when she finally died, his grief would be softened by the knowledge that his mother was with God in Heaven. This would not make him miss her any more, but it would make him happy to know that she was with his Friend the Lord Jesus.

Finally the day came when Faun wrote to Doctor John saying,

'Thank you so much for praying for me and my mother. She has just died, but a few days before she died she told me that she too loved God, and because of our talks together she had asked the Lord Jesus to forgive all her wrong, and I know she is with Him in Heaven now.'

Faun's life was bleak and meaningless without his mother. She had always been at the centre. He now had no purpose left. Sometimes he could not stop crying in bed at night for his mother, athough he knew that crying could never bring her back again.

He stayed on with his granny, learning her great skills in making Thai cookies, and then taking them to the market to sell. She was a clever Thai cake-maker. However, his granny had always been a half-stranger to him, and besides that, she did not really want him to go on believing in Jesus. It would have been much simpler for her to have a Buddhist grandson to bring up. Faun could understand just how she must feel about it.

'God — whatever is going to happen to me?' he often prayed when he was alone in bed at night under his mosquito net, lying on his mat on the wooden floor. The flickering oil lamp danced and traced fascinating patterns on the wooden walls, but these no longer intrigued Faun. He was lonely. He was cut off from his friends at Manorom, and from his school friends. The

Faun's Granny was happy to take him to Manorom.

light reminded him of Jesus who had said that He was the Light of the world. Although Faun's world seemed black, he believed that somehow everything would work out all right and that Jesus would not abandon him now.

Then, right out of the blue, his granny received a most surprising letter that neither he nor she had anticipated. The letter said that before she had died, his mother had asked that the medical superintendent of Manorom

Hospital should be responsible for Faun's education. (They did not know it, but this had been at Doctor John's suggestion.) It seemed that the doctor and Faun's mother must have talked about this together and agreed to it.

Faun's granny was happy to take him to Manorom. While she would gladly have brought him up, this boy with his strange religion was a puzzle to her.

They went to see Doctor John immediately. 'Faun,' said the doctor, looking him straight in the eye, 'you'll have to try your hardest now. We've managed to get you a place in one of the very best Christian schools that is up-country and not in Bangkok. As you've come top every term in your old school, we're going to send you to a bigger school . . . and if you do well there, then you'll have the chance to do almost anything you want with your life. This school can give you all the teaching that you'll need for anything.'

Faun did not know what to say. He had heard of this school, but had never thought that a boy like him would ever be able to go there. Here was a chance to keep his promise to his mother to make something worthwhile of his life.

'But,' Doctor John had not finished all he had to say — 'we are going to have to do something together. I haven't enough money to pay for your schooling myself, so you and we Townsends will have to trust God together that every term He will send you the money needed for school fees and uniform.'

Faun felt a huge lump rise in his throat. Once before, God had sent him money in answer to prayer. It had been years earlier, when he had needed money to save Jon's life . . . and it made him remember his old friend, the naughtiest pig. But this God who had sent the money to save Jon surely would not let Faun down now. The same God would surely do the same thing for him?

Very few people knew of the existence of a small Thai boy called Faun, and even less of his need of money for schooling. Faun and the Townsends regularly prayed that God would send the money needed for Faun's schooling . . . and He did. Each term one or two people who knew about Faun were moved by God to send the money needed for him to go to school and to have all the clothes and other things that the other children had. He did not have to go without anything.

He began to go regularly to Manorom for the school holidays and stayed with a Thai Christian family, where he was welcomed as an elder brother to the son and daughter of the house.

He was there the exciting day when the headmaster came a long way to visit the hospital and Doctor John. He had noticed his Thai headmaster's familiar red car whizzing down the hospital drive, and had followed it to the Townsends' house.

He stood shyly by as the headmaster announced to Doctor John, 'Faun's come top of his class for the year!' and blushed with pride, staring hard at his shoes.

The headmaster then made a forgetful blunder, 'What does your mother think of the news?' he asked, obviously forgetting for the time being that Faun now had no mother.

Quick as a flash, Faun turned to Doctor Anne, 'She's my new mother, ask her,' he said simply and politely.

With those words he knew that he now belonged somewhere. He belonged in a Thai family and Christian home. He belonged to a Christian school and was making the grade there. At Manorom he belonged to the group of people who had known and loved his mother and who now loved him especially because of her. Best of all he belonged to the kind of God who he knew would never let him down or leave him alone.

He was given little time to think. Small Christopher came running up to him, 'Please take me for a walk in the rice fields. Mummy says I can't go alone, but I can go with you . . .'

He took the small hand into his own.

He not only belonged, he was needed and wanted.

He took the small hand into his own.